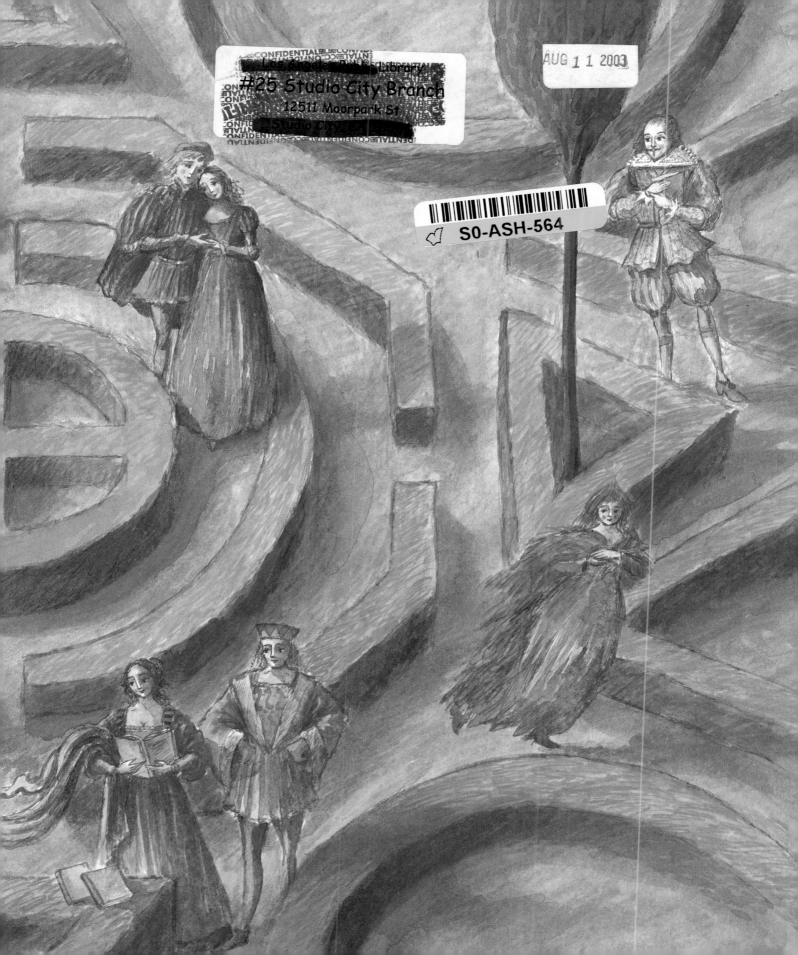

For my parents, Mick and Fran
~ P.R. ~
For Max and Eloise, from your Uncle
~ J.M. ~

Shakespeare's Storybook

Barefoot Books
37 West 17th Street
4th Floor East
New York, NY 10011

This book was typeset in Janson Text 13pt on 18pt leading
Illustrations were prepared in watercolor and pen and ink on watercolor paper

Graphic design by designsection, Frome, England
Color separation by Grafiscan, Verona, Italy
Printed and bound in Hong Kong by South China Printing Co. (1988) Ltd

This book has been printed on 100% acid-free paper

Library of Congress Cataloging-in-Publication Data

Ryan, Patrick, 1948-
    Shakespeare's storybook : folk tales that inspired the bard /
retold by Patrick Ryan ; illustrated by James Mayhew.
        p. cm.
    The Devil's Bet / The Taming of the Shrew — The Hill of Roses /
Romeo and Juliet — A Bargain is a Bargain / The Merchant of Venice —
Snowdrop / As You Like It — Ashboy / Hamlet — Cap-O-Rushes / King
Lear — The Flower Princess / The Winter's Tale.
    ISBN 1 84148 307 9
    1. Shakespeare, William, 1564-1616—Sources—Juvenile literature.
2. Folklore—Juvenile literature. [1. Shakespeare, William,
1564-1616—Sources. 2. Folklore.]   I. Mayhew, James, 1964-   . ill.
II. Title.
    PR2952.5 R93 2001
    822.3'3—dc21
    2001000237

1 3 5 7 9 8 6 4 2

Shakespeare's Storybook

~FOLK TALES THAT INSPIRED THE BARD~

Retold by
PATRICK RYAN

Illustrated by
JAMES MAYHEW

Barefoot Books
better books for children

✦CONTENTS✦

·Introduction·

A storyteller knows that a good story is worth telling more than once. And any storyteller can tell you that each time a tale is told, it may be a little different and a little better than it was before. Storytellers will also say that how a story is told depends on the listeners. The story will be told to suit their ears. An audience can affect a story in different ways, shaping it and changing it.

William Shakespeare was one of the best storytellers in the world. He knew a good story when he heard one, and he recognized a good story when he read it. Shakespeare was also a brilliant poet, who wrote words of great power and beauty, and had a special way of looking at the world. But he did not usually make up the stories that he told. He took popular stories and made them into poems and plays.

Sometimes he wrote a play so that it followed the story exactly as he first heard or read it. Sometimes he changed the story to make a completely new version. Not only did he know a good story, he knew which stories his audiences would enjoy, and wrote plays to please his listeners. Shakespeare also knew that audiences of his day would show their feelings, cheering the parts they liked. If they didn't like certain parts, they would show their feelings, too, but in a way that wasn't very pleasant for the actors!

In Shakespeare's time, during the late 1500s, public theaters were brand new. Not only were they new buildings, they were an entirely new idea. As far as we know, there were no specially built theaters in Britain before that time. Those buildings that had plays performed in them were owned by noblemen or the church, and they were used mostly for events besides entertainment. If a nobleman paid for a play to be performed, it was seen only by his friends and his retainers (those who worked for him). If the church paid for a play, it was usually a sacred work, which taught the community the stories of the Bible and the lessons that churchmen wanted the people in their parishes to learn.

Many of the performers for these events were local people, not full-time, professional actors. Some of them did perform for a living – as minstrels, musicians, bards, acrobats and storytellers. They could be performers who traveled around, but usually they were retainers, in the employment of a nobleman. To make extra money, they put on shows in the courtyards of inns and public houses, which were gradually turned into public theaters.

When Shakespeare started working, theaters were opening to the public for the first time, to anyone who could pay, and not just to those invited by a nobleman or those who churchmen wanted to teach. The actors, or players, became the first professional performers.

Printing, and printed books and pamphlets, had only been around since the late 1400s. The printing press, and printed books, seemed as new, exciting and useful to people then as computers seem to us now. Before public theaters and printing presses were invented, people entertained one another by telling stories, reciting poetry from memory, reading aloud from handwritten books and singing songs called ballads, which told stories. Sometimes these performers were people who lived and worked in the community, but who had a talent for storytelling. Sometimes they were performers who traveled from place to place, such as ballad singers, minstrels, bards and troubadours.

So when these newfangled inventions (printed books and theaters) came into being, people thought of them in terms of the stories and songs that they were used to hearing in taverns and in their homes. Nowadays we would say that we're going to "see" a play. The people in Tudor times used to say that they were going to "hear" a play.

Shakespeare must have listened to stories all his life. He read everything he could lay his hands on. And those stories he heard and read were turned into marvelous plays – plays that still tell wonderful stories today.

The audiences in Shakespeare's time knew the stories, books and poems that he based his plays upon. But today most people have forgotten them. We only know the stories because we know Shakespeare's plays: those are the only versions of the tales that are left. Or at least that's what most people think.

But if you look at old books, and listen to storytellers who continue to tell tales in the traditional way that the bards and minstrels did, you can find the stories in forms like those in which Shakespeare first heard them. Some of these stories have been hunted down and retold here.

Maybe Shakespeare heard these tales from his mother, or his grandfather, or his teachers. Perhaps he told these tales to his own children. And, of course, he would have heard stories in the public houses, and from his friends, and told stories back to them. In his day, London grew famous for its theaters and booksellers, so people came to the city from all over Europe; they brought tales from every corner of the world with them, and Shakespeare would have heard these stories, too. Luckily for us, he liked the stories so much that he adapted them and created his unforgettable plays and poems.

So enjoy the stories in this book. As you read them, remember that there is no one standard version of each tale. Each story has many different sources – some told orally, some written down. The stories have changed and evolved from teller to teller. Shakespeare is just one more yarn spinner who belongs to this grand tradition.

People have loved hearing these stories, and reading them, and telling them and retelling them, for hundreds of years. When you've had fun with them, maybe you'll retell them in your own way, and do an even better job than William Shakespeare did!

Patrick Ryan

THE·DEVIL'S·BET

The Taming of the Shrew

One of Shakespeare's earliest plays is *The Taming of the Shrew*, which he wrote in about 1592. The play tells of a young woman, named Katherina, who no one wants to marry because she has such a bad temper. Petruchio takes up the challenge to marry her and teach her how to be kind so she can get what she wishes from life.

People in fairy tales fall in love and live happily ever after. That does not always happen in real life. Being married happily ever after is hard work. Many folk tales are about the troubles husbands and wives have – their quarrels and the tricks they play on each other. In some versions, the husband torments the wife, and in others, the wife torments the husband. Some stories suggest that being kind and thoughtful toward each other is a better route to lasting happiness than quarreling and fighting.

KATHERINA

The most unusual version, retold here, involves an intriguing monster – a water demon or devil – who keeps playing tricks on the wife because of her bad temper. The story is drawn from a number of sources, mostly Irish, and some Welsh and English. Many stories from these countries tell of spirits, fairies, demons and devils living in running streams and stagnant pools. The Nicky Nicky Nye is actually found in Wales, and is a Gwent

PETRUCHIO

river spirit. What is interesting about "The Devil's Bet" is that it brings together the water spirit theme with that of the sparring husband and wife.

Shakespeare's *The Taming of the Shrew* is based on similar stories. Because there would have been so many folk tales, ballads and broadsheets relating this popular yarn during his day, it is difficult to know exactly which version he used. Shakespeare set his story in Italy, but there are a couple of clues in the play itself, which suggest that he based it on an Irish or British story. For a start, the action begins at an alehouse on a heath. Yet heaths and alehouses are a feature of the British Isles, not of Italy. In the play, the lords and ladies visiting the pub play a trick on a drunken tinker and treat him as a king. But tinkers do not come from Italy either. They were Irish and Scottish travelers, called "tinkers" (although it was a name they did not like) because in those days they earned a living, as they moved around the country, by making things out of tin.

The main message of the play, that a "good match of equals" is important in marriage, is something that Shakespeare himself believed in. While he worked in London, his wife Anne raised their children and kept their business interests going in Stratford. She did so well that they were able to make as much money from her work as they did from Shakespeare's writing. It seems that in old age they did settle down to live happily together.

NICKY NICKY NYE

THE·DEVIL'S·BET

There was a widow who had a daughter named Nora. Nora was beautiful, but very grumpy and terribly lazy. She never lifted a finger to help and never had a kind word. Spoiled and quarrelsome, Nora always had her own way.

In the forest nearby lived a woodsman called Jamie. He had a comfortable, pretty cottage and wanted someone to share it with. There was just one problem. In the spring by his home dwelled the Nicky Nicky Nye, a wicked water devil. This did not worry Jamie, for the devil only came out at night. And why should it worry his wife-to-be? What bother is a demon if a woodsman and his wife each have a good strong spirit?

Jamie saddled his donkey and went in search of a wife – a sparky young woman he could fall in love with. He hadn't gone far when he came upon the widow's daughter.

Nora was sitting by the river, dirty laundry scattered all about her. Her mother had sent her to do the washing. Instead she sat and daydreamed, while the clothes drifted in the tide.

Jamie asked a passing farmer, "Who is that beauty, and has she a sweetheart?"

"That's Nora!" laughed the farmer. "Nasty Nora they call her. No one could ever love her."

"I could," declared the woodsman. "With all my heart."

"Well, good luck," the farmer replied. "She's so contrary she gives her poor mother nothing but grief. The widow tries to keep things tidy, but Nora always makes a mess."

"All the more reason to marry me!" smiled Jamie. "She can come to live in my pretty cottage. Tidy or messy, I don't mind." He began to move away.

"Hang on – I've more to tell you!" continued the farmer. "Her mother sent Nora to buy food for supper, and the selfish girl spent the money on ribbons for her hair!"

"So, a woman who needs little to eat," laughed Jamie. "All the better for me – and what pretty hair to tie up with ribbons!"

So saying, he went up to Nora and spoke ever so politely. "Pretty maiden, your fine clothes will soon be washed away in the tide. Permit me to help fetch them back."

"Do what you like!" sniffed Nora.

"Very well," laughed Jamie. "I'll be glad to help."

With that, he picked Nora up – which she liked very much, for he was a strong, handsome fellow. Then he threw her in the river – which she didn't like at all.

"There you go!" he cried. "You'll catch the clothes easily enough, now that you're in the water!"

Spluttering and swearing, gasping and moaning, Nora gathered up the garments and stomped back to the bank.

"And you needn't mind getting wet," Jamie told her. "The water will wash away all your grumpiness."

Cursing, she threw the wet things in Jamie's face.

"Whoa, Nora," cried Jamie. "Is that how to treat your sweetheart?"

"What sweetheart?" shrieked Nora. "I'll never be sweet to you!"

"Oh, you will," Jamie promised. "You and I are getting married today!"

With that, he took Nora by the arm and escorted her to her mother. The widow looked so tired and sad that Jamie resolved to marry Nora at once. Then the mother would be able to live in peace, and perhaps learn to smile again.

Jamie sat down and told them of his cottage in the wood, and the garden all around with songbirds singing and bees humming. It all sounded so lovely – for he made no mention of the water devil lurking in the well. Nora agreed that she was tired of living with her mother. She fancied life in a pretty cottage of her own, especially with a handsome husband like Jamie, with his curly black hair. True, he had played a trick on her – but couldn't she play tricks, too? They might be well matched.

So they went to the church to get married. Jamie and the widow were in such a hurry, Nora had no time to change out of her wet clothes. She had no time to celebrate, either, for Jamie whisked her away straight after the wedding.

"We must hurry and get back before dark," Jamie explained, as they trotted along on the donkey into the thick, dark wood. He wanted to be indoors before the demon showed itself.

"This donkey's too slow, too lumpy, too bumpy to move quickly," grumbled Nora. "Why don't you beat him with your stick?"

"Beat my dear donkey?" exclaimed Jamie. "No, no, no, that would never do."

"Why not?" asked Nora. "It would make him go faster."

Jamie only replied, "I have found, my dear, that soft words and a gentle touch win more than harsh words and mean tricks."

As night fell, they came to the pretty cottage. Jamie's dog rushed out to greet them, barking and jumping for joy, and splattering them with mud from head to toe.

"The dirty beast!" screamed Nora. "That dog's too loud, his paws are too muddy, his tongue's too wet! Why don't you beat him with your stick?"

"Beat my dear doggie?" exclaimed Jamie. "No, no, no, that would never do."

"Why not?" asked Nora. "It would make him behave."

But Jamie only replied, "I have found, my dear, that soft words and a gentle touch win more than harsh words and mean tricks."

Then he opened the door of the cottage, and in they went.

"Nora, dear darling, I'm so thirsty," said Jamie as they stepped inside. "Please make us a pot of tea while I fetch more wood for the fire."

"I'm not your servant!" snapped Nora, her eyes blazing. "And here's to your pot of tea!"

With these angry words, she smashed the china teapot on the floor, adding cheekily, "Where do soft words and a gentle touch get you now?"

"I suppose I deserved that for dropping you in the river," said Jamie. "But your harsh words and mean tricks have hurt you as much as me. Without a teapot, there'll be no tea for either of us!"

Before Nora could reply, there was a rumble of laughter from the well. Up out of the water jumped the demon, and through the window popped the head of the Nicky Nicky Nye.

"Ho, ho, ho," he laughed. "Jamie, who have you there?"

"My wife, Nora," Jamie answered proudly.

"A wife!" roared the devil. "She'll not stay long – not with me about!"

"Who says I'll not stay?" shouted Nora.

"I do!" snapped the demon. "The Nicky Nicky Nye! You'll not last a week with me around."

"I bet I will!" snarled Nora, gritting her teeth. "No one chases me away."

"Right," said the Nicky Nicky Nye. "The bet's on. I'll bet all the gold and silver hidden in my well I can drive you away before the week is out!"

"Done," said Nora. "But it's you who'll be going."

"We'll see!" grinned the water devil. "And if you lose the bet – I'll gobble you up as you try to run away!"

Then the Nicky Nicky Nye sank back into the well, and Jamie's smiling face turned glum.

"Oh dear, dear," he said. "Nora, what have you done? I don't want the Nicky Nicky Nye to gobble you up."

"He won't!" said Nora determinedly. "I'll see to him!"

"Just remember," begged her husband, "soft words and a gentle touch win more than harsh words and mean tricks."

Between Nora and the demon it was war. The water devil only came out at night, but Nora couldn't escape him. Every time she entered the garden, the Nicky Nicky Nye would throw at her the foulest stuff from nearby ponds and streams – scum and duckweed, mud and sludge. Dripping with slime, Nora would try to get back at him by dumping the dirty dishwater into the well, or emptying the chamber pot onto the demon's head. But he only spat it back in her face.

It went on like this each day until, finally, Nora could bear it no more. She no longer cared for the pretty cottage or even her handsome black-haired husband. She just wanted to run away – then remembered that, if she did, the Nicky Nicky Nye would gobble her up.

"Harsh words and mean tricks won't win," Jamie reminded her. "Soft words and a gentle touch are what do the job best."

The last night had arrived and Nora was all ready to flee. But Jamie's advice came back to her and at last gave her an idea. She packed a basket of food, as if ready to leave, then came to stand by the well.

"Ha ha!" laughed the demon when he saw her. "I've won the bet! You're running away – get ready to be gobbled up!"

"You're quite wrong, my darling little demon," Nora smiled. "I'm not running away. It's such a lovely day I thought I'd go for a stroll in the garden."

"You're mad!" said the water devil. "It's the middle of the night."

"No," disagreed Nora. "Just look at the bright, blinding sun!"

"That's the moon!" roared the devil.

"No, it's the sun," grinned Nora. "And I'm so worried to see you out and about in the daylight."

"It's not daylight!" shouted the water devil. "It's moonlight!"

Nora ignored him. "And you never come out in the day, only in the night. I fear you may soon shrivel up!"

"I don't need your concern," grumbled the Nicky Nicky Nye.

"So I made you some sweet, refreshing lemonade," said Nora, as she opened the basket and brought out a bottle.

"I hate lemonade!" shouted the devil. "Leave me alone!"

But Nora would not let the demon be. She smothered him with kindness. She charmed him with soft words, and plied him with lemonade and cakes, cookies and sweets. The Nicky Nicky Nye could not bear it.

"I think I'm going to be sick!" he cried.

"There, there," Nora soothed. "As my husband says, a soft word and a gentle touch will take care of that."

And she gave the Nicky Nicky Nye a pat on the head. The monster was so overcome by all this kindness he truly could not bear it. He huffed and puffed and blew himself up bigger and bigger and bigger – until he burst.

And that was the end of the water demon. Never again did he bother the woodsman and his wife. Deep down at the bottom of the well, Jamie and Nora found the Nicky Nicky Nye's hoard of gold and silver, which, of course, they kept for themselves. Nora had won the devil's bet, after all. From that time on, she and Jamie tried to get by as best they could – with soft words and a gentle touch.

THE·HILL·OF·ROSES

Romeo and Juliet

The tale of Romeo and Juliet is, perhaps, the best-known love story in all the world. It is also one of Shakespeare's most popular plays, and one of his first tragedies. The play, written in 1595, tells of two young people who live in Verona, a town in Italy. Their families hate each other, but they disobey their parents, fall in love, and get married secretly. The young lovers hope that their union will bring peace, but it is not until the death of Romeo and Juliet that the two families finally agree to get along together.

Love stories are always popular, even when they are sad. Many similar versions of the tale of Romeo and Juliet existed well before Shakespeare made the story into a play. In fact, one version, the story of Pyramis and Thisbe, was used by Shakespeare in his comedy *A Midsummer Night's Dream*. Using comic characters, he tells the story of Pyramis and Thisbe in a very funny way, making a joke out of the manner in which some actors perform tragic love stories.

We believe that Shakespeare based *Romeo and Juliet* on a poem called The *Tragicall Historye of Romeus and Juliet*, translated and adapted by Arthur Brooke from a French work in 1562. He could also have found an account of the young lovers in William Painter's *Palace of Pleasure* (1566), a book containing many stories Shakespeare later made into plays. The story retold here looks to both these sources, but also draws upon a similar love story by Bernard Garter, *The Tragicall and True*

ROMEO

Historie which Happened between Two English Lovers (1563), and an ancient Scottish folk tale, "The Stone of Roses". But the main source is *Il Novellino* by Salernitano Masuccio (1474), one of the oldest written accounts of the love story, and one which Shakespeare, too, may have known.

However, many people believe that the story of Romeo and Juliet is, in fact, a true tale of two feuding families from medieval Verona. There were, long ago in that part of Italy, people with the same surnames as those of the lovers' two families. To this day, people go to Verona to visit the house that is thought to have belonged to Juliet's family. You can even see the balcony where Romeo was supposed to have courted Juliet!

Whether true or not, the story has always been popular. Even Puritan preachers, church ministers, teachers and priests approved of the tale and used it in their sermons. They thought it taught a good lesson, warning young people to behave themselves and not to disobey their parents. It could even be that Shakespeare first heard the story in a Sunday sermon, except that he recognized, of course, that the tale isn't really about obedience, but about how love can break down barriers that should never have been put there in the first place.

JULIET

and known too late!" I v

THE·HILL·OF·ROSES

Far away in a distant land there is a hill completely covered with roses. There is an old story of how the hill came to be that way, but it is hardly ever told. Some say it's a tale too sad for the telling.

In ancient times, two villages stood on either side of that hill. The people of each village were sworn enemies. They would have nothing to do with each other, and there was no business between them. When troubled times came, the villagers of one hamlet refused to help those of the other. When good times returned, the two villages never celebrated together. There was never any love between the two villages, only hatred.

The hill that separated these hamlets became a kind of no man's land. In time it became the only thing the villages shared, for both used the hill as a graveyard for their dead.

Now in one village, there lived a man called Romeus. He was young and reckless. Some called him brave, others said he was crazy. He was always doing wild things to show off to his friends.

In the other village was a young woman named Julietta, who lived with Tibbot, her brother.

"Julietta's the most beautiful girl in the world!" That's what everyone claimed. Even the people in Romeus' village had to admit she was lovely.

So one midwinter, when Julietta and Tibbot's father announced he would be hosting a fancy dress ball, everyone wanted to go. Even the men of Romeus' village, who were enemies of Julietta's people, wanted to go so they could see her. But no one dared.

"How I wish I could take a look at this Julietta!" sighed Quicksilver, Romeus' best friend.

"I'll go and look at her," boasted Romeus. "After all, who's to know? The party is fancy dress!"

"Then I dare you!" Quicksilver teased, never dreaming that Romeus would.

The crazy boy disguised himself, dressing up as a nymph so no one would recognize him. Carefully climbing the hill, he found his way down the path that wound into Julietta's village, and slipped into the ballroom. He was dressed up, so no one knew that he wasn't a local.

At the first chance, Romeus grabbed Julietta's arm and swept her into a dance. His hands felt warm, while everyone else's had been freezing!

"Thank you for the dance," smiled Julietta as she curtsied to him. "And for giving me your warm hands – for they've warmed mine."

It was then they looked into each other's eyes, and fell in love. When Romeus left the ball, Julietta followed him. She paused when she saw him entering the graveyard to climb the hill. Could she have fallen in love with a ghost? Even so, that love made her follow Romeus up the path. Seeing him head down the other side of the hill, she realized he came from the village of her enemies. Even so, she called, "Wait, please, wait!"

Romeus stopped. When he turned and saw Julietta, he hurried back to her, took her by hand again, and they kissed. For a long while they stood in the cold winter's moonlight talking and talking, as if they would never stop. When at last they parted, they had planned to meet again.

"Whenever we can and wish to meet, let us send each other a rose," said Julietta. And Romeus agreed.

So it was that each week, sometimes each day, Romeus would send a red rose, plucked from the glasshouse in his garden, or Julietta would send a white rose, carefully cultivated in the sheltered cloisters of her village church. That was a sign that one of them would be at the top of the hill in the evening. And the other would always be there, with a warm welcome.

Their love grew. But they dared not tell anyone about it, even family or friends. Romeus and Julietta hoped they might get married, and so bring their people together. As winter passed and songbirds began to return to welcome in the spring, they promised each other that soon they would find a way to wed.

Time passed, and the people of each village grew to hate each other more than ever. Many feared the two places would each be destroyed, and everyone killed. Tibbot, Julietta's own brother, was one of those most full of hate. He was ever watchful, always looking for signs of his enemies and itching to pick a fight. It wasn't long before he became suspicious of Julietta's quiet and secret ways. He began to follow her, suspecting that his own sister had betrayed him and his friends by falling in love with one of the enemy.

One spring night, as Romeus and Julietta walked arm in arm atop the hill, the snow began to fall. So cold and heavy was the unseasonable blizzard that Romeus begged Julietta to let him take her safely back to her house, where he would spend the night, or to return with him to his home.

"We can't do that!" gasped Julietta. "We can't spend the night together under one roof until we're married."

"Then let's marry tonight!" Romeus pleaded. Julietta looked into his eyes and agreed at once.

They raced through the snow to the little church by the graveyard, and knocked loudly at the door to wake the friar. This holy man had long prayed that the villages would stop their fighting. When he had listened to the young people and learned of their eagerness to be wed, he agreed to marry them, for he hoped that this would put an end to the quarrel.

That night was the happiest Romeus and Julietta had ever known. They woke, in Julietta's house, to the sound of a nightingale singing in harmony with a lark. The snowstorm of the night before had melted away, and Romeus carefully made his way home. That day each would tell their fellow villagers of the marriage that had taken place. If the people would not join together to celebrate their happiness, then he and Julietta would run away together to make a new life somewhere else.

But it was too late. As Romeus approached his village, he found it under attack. Julietta's brother, Tibbot, had seen them on the hill the night before, and now knew for certain that his sister loved one of the enemy. In his fury he had led a gang of angry young men around the hill to burn down the neighboring village. He wanted to destroy it completely and save his sister from her folly. But Quicksilver, always on the lookout for trouble, had seen Tibbot and his men approach with flaming torches in their hands. He roused his people at once to fight the gang and save their homes.

This was the mad scene that greeted Romeus as he entered his village. He ran at once into the fray. "Stop!" he screamed. "Stop the fighting!"

Just at that moment, Quicksilver dashed at Tibbot with his sword. Romeus pushed his friend away, hoping to save the brother of his wife. But Tibbot was too quick: as Quicksilver fell, Tibbot stabbed him with his dagger, killing him at once.

"Murderer!" cried Romeus, mad with grief. Seizing Quicksilver's sword, he lunged at Tibbot. Single-handedly, he drove out Tibbot and all his men, sending them back to their village.

Back at home, Tibbot told his sister the grim news, watching her to see what she would do.

Julietta wept with fear. "And how was Romeus, when you left him?" she begged to know.

"You snake-in-the-grass!" roared Tibbot. "You do love him!"

"We were married last night," Julietta admitted through her tears. "He's my husband now."

"Never," spat Tibbot. "You're lying! You'll never be married to him! You'll marry a man of this village – you'll marry who I say! You will marry the first man I bring back to this house!"

With that, Tibbot went out to fetch a man, any man, to force on his beautiful sister, whom he now hated more than anything in the world.

Julietta ran at once to the friar and told of all the disasters that had occurred. "What am I to do?" she cried. "I can't get to Romeus in time, and I dare not stay with my brother!"

"First, we must try to calm everyone down," replied the friar. "When all is quiet, then everything can be sorted out. We must try to make peace."

"But how?" Julietta implored. "The only peace these villages know is the peace that comes with death."

This gave the priest his plan. Along with his wisdom and his many skills, the friar possessed some magic. He told Julietta of a certain potion. If taken, this potion would make a person appear to be dead when, truly, he slept only a very deep sleep from which he would awaken after three days.

"Let me drink this potion!" Julietta insisted. "When Tibbot thinks I'm dead, my people will bury me. You then can make the peace. If you cannot, send a white rose to my husband with a message that he is to meet me at my tomb, and take me away to a place where we can love each other in freedom."

The friar agreed to all this. Julietta drank the potion and collapsed to the floor of the church. The priest raised the alarm, and when Tibbot came he was told the news.

"You see what you have done?" said the friar with great sadness. "Your beautiful sister has died of a broken heart."

There was much weeping and wailing then. Tibbot ordered that all fighting should cease for a while, out of respect for his sister. A funeral was arranged, and a grand tomb built, and Julietta was placed within.

Throughout the funeral, the friar begged Tibbot to make peace. But Tibbot refused, promising instead, "When my sister's buried, we'll destroy those who broke her heart!"

So the friar had no choice but to pluck a white rose from the church cloister and tie to it a message for Romeus:

> *Your true love is not dead ~ she waits for you and wishes a new life for you both. Meet her at her tomb.*

This was sent at once to Romeus. That night he eagerly climbed the hill to meet his love. But guarding the tomb was Tibbot, who rushed at Romeus with his sword. At once the two were fighting, tooth and nail. Tibbot's grief made him stronger, and before long, Romeus fell to the ground – dead.

At that moment, the tomb opened and Julietta, now awake, stepped out. At the sight of her husband lying dead at Tibbot's feet, she flew at her brother, crying, "You've killed him! You've killed him! For this you'll pay dearly!"

Tibbot went pale with shock and almost fainted. He had believed his sister dead, and thought this must be her ghost come back to haunt him.

"Julietta, forgive me!" he begged, falling to his knees. "Tell me what to do so you won't curse me!"

"Make peace between the villages," Julietta commanded. "And never try to see me again."

Shaking with fear, Tibbot turned and fled. Never truly understanding what had happened, but fearing his sister, whether dead or alive, he made sure that peace between the villages came at last.

Romeus was buried by his friends in the grave meant for Julietta. Julietta remained in the tomb with her dead husband. She would not leave, longing only for her own death.

The friar, horrified at how everything had gone so wrong, pleaded with Julietta to leave the graveyard and live again among her people. But she refused. She made the tomb a holy place, where she lived as a hermit. And not long after the death of her beloved Romeus, she died of a broken heart. The friar placed her in the tomb, beside Romeus.

The sad story of what had happened was told throughout the land. Everyone came to know the tale. Many people whose hearts had been ruined by love came to see the place for themselves. From that time on, the people of both villages planted roses on that hill: red ones and white ones. Roses in memory of those who had died for love. Roses to remind the villagers of the true cost of hatred, and the price of peace. And even to this day the hill is covered with roses – red blooms all mingled with white.

PORTIA: "The words expressly are

A·BARGAIN·IS·A·BARGAIN

The Merchant of Venice

The *Merchant of Venice*, written between 1596 and 1598, tells how Antonio borrows money from Shylock, a merchant and Jew. This is to help his friend Bassanio marry the beautiful Portia by solving a puzzle involving three "caskets", or boxes made out of wood. Shylock's daughter runs away to marry a Christian, and her father is so angry that when Antonio does not pay back the money on time, Shylock insists that he pay with a pound of flesh. Portia helps to solve the terrible problem.

Shakespeare used two different folk stories to create his play. He based the main plot – the loan of money and the payment of flesh – on a story from *Il Pecorone*, a collection of tales written by Giovanni Fiorentino around 1378. The theme of the caskets is based on an early variant of "The Princess and the Pea", which Shakespeare would have found in the medieval *Gesta Romanorum*, a collection of short stories that influenced many writers.

"A Bargain is a Bargain" is based on the oldest rendition of the story of the pound of flesh, "Dolopathos and the Seven Wise Men", which probably came to Europe from the Orient during the time of the Crusades. My retelling also borrows much from Giovanni's story and the *Gesta Romanorum* tales.

In the folk tale versions of the story, the bargain is usually made between two close friends or family

SHYLOCK

Take then thou bond,

members. In choosing a Jewish merchant as the one who loans the money and demands a pound of flesh, Shakespeare may have had in mind a couple of incidents, supposedly true, that happened in his time. The first concerns a Jewish merchant in Italy who lost a bet with a bishop friend of his, and might have had to pay with a pound of flesh if the Pope had not come to his rescue. After this, all the folk versions of the story changed, so that the one demanding the pound of flesh was always portrayed as a Jewish merchant and moneylender. In the Middle Ages, and even in Shakespeare's day, the Christian church did not permit Christians to lend money. So it was one business that Jews could run – but they were not very popular for providing this service. This may be another reason why the lender in the tale was portrayed as Jewish.

PORTIA

The second incident concerns an act of revenge against another Jew. Elizabeth I had a doctor named Lopez, a Portuguese Jew, who refused to help the Earl of Essex in his plot to betray the queen. The earl was so popular that people believed him when he said that Lopez had tried to poison the queen, and so the loyal doctor was hanged for treason. Shakespeare might well have known Dr. Lopez. He almost certainly knew what the earl had done, for the Earl of Essex even attempted to get Shakespeare's theater company to help in his plot to destroy the queen. Eventually the earl was caught and punished. It is quite likely that Shakespeare took what he knew about these true stories and mixed them with the folk tales to make his famous play.

Elizabeth I

ANTONIO

A·BARGAIN·IS·A·BARGAIN

There was once a rich merchant who had two sons. These brothers were as different as the crow and the peacock, or as the moon and the sun, or as hot and cold. The elder, serious and somber, cared only for money. The younger was friendly and warm, always joking and often foolish.

Their old father was ill. He knew his time had come and called his sons to his side. "My boys," said the merchant, "I'm close to death. All my life I have worked hard, built a business, made a fortune. I leave all that to you. Now tell me, what will you each do with my money?"

The older son promised to use his inheritance wisely and keep the family business going.

But did the younger boy say, "Father, I'm going to be just like you – a great businessman"? No, he did not. Instead he said, "Father, I'm going to spend your money! I'm going to have a good time! I'll buy fancy clothes, good food and wine. I'll have music, and dancing, and beautiful women around me always!"

These words broke his father's heart, and the old man died in that instant.

The older brother became ever more serious, and wisely invested the fortune left to him. Soon, he was even more successful than his father had been.

And the younger brother did just as he had promised. He went on a spree. He dressed in expensive clothes of the latest fashion. He flirted with young women, and hired musicians so he could hear sweet melodies all the time. He didn't

30

even think about work. He feasted on the finest food, drank the best wine and held wild parties.

Soon he had spent all his fortune. Penniless, he found his friends soon left him. They were the kind who only stick with someone who has money. The young man was homeless, dressed in rags. Living in the street, he became a beggar. People said it was shameful. The older brother was disgusted with his younger brother. But the young man didn't mind being poor. He seemed perfectly happy.

Now, the duke of that city had a daughter who was both beautiful and wise. Many men asked to marry her. But she had no desire to wed, for she loved only books and stories, thoughts and ideas. She turned down all of the men and spent her days reading.

Even so, men pestered her, and the duke demanded she choose a husband. So his daughter devised a test. She gave orders for three caskets to be made: the first of gold, the second of silver and the last of wood. She declared that if any man could solve the puzzle and choose the casket that held the prize worth having, he would be her husband. Many tried to solve the puzzle, but all failed.

So the duke's daughter happily continued her peaceful existence – absorbed in her books. The only distractions that could tempt her away from the palace, and her beloved books, were the fun-filled festivals and lively carnivals for which her city was famed.

One day, when carnival was in full swing, the younger brother caught sight of the duke's daughter. He fell in love at once, and was determined to solve the puzzle and marry her.

But how could he appear before her in rags? Could a beggar marry the daughter of a duke? It seemed impossible, but this young man was relentless. He went to his brother and asked for some money.

"Why should I give money to you, you scoundrel?" grumbled the older brother.

"Because, dear brother," the younger man lied, "I'm so sorry for my foolishness and wickedness. I want to make amends. I want to be like you and Father. Give me some money, so I can prove myself and be a merchant."

His brother didn't believe him. He wouldn't part with any of his money, not a single penny.

"Then loan me the money, brother!" he pleaded. "With the carnival on, I can sell many things. I'm sure to make a great fortune!"

"What if you fail and can't pay me back?" asked the older brother.

"If I can't pay with money," the younger one swore, "I'll pay with anything you want – just name it!"

"You've nothing! Nothing but your own flesh!" exclaimed his exasperated brother.

"Then I'll pay with that," he announced. "If I can't pay with money, I shall pay with my own flesh."

"Very well," agreed his brother. "I'll loan the amount you ask for. If you can't pay me back by the end of carnival, then I'll cut away a pound of flesh from the place closest to your heart."

A bargain was made, a deal done, an agreement settled upon. Documents were drawn up, and the contract signed and witnessed. The younger brother took the money, never dreaming he would have to pay it back. "My brother will be so proud when I'm married to the duke's daughter, he'll not care about the money," he thought to himself.

Certainly, he never believed his brother would cut away a pound of his flesh – that was just a jest. But the brother was deadly serious, and determined to punish the younger man, if necessary, to teach him a lesson.

Rather than spend the money on goods to sell at carnival, the young man had the finest clothes made up. Dressed in the latest fashion, he cut a fine figure. One would have thought he was a prince, or even an emperor. He went to the palace and demanded that the duke's daughter put him to the test.

The young man was taken at once to her chamber, where the three caskets sat. He was asked to choose the one that held the prize worth having. Carefully, he read the inscription on each casket.

The golden casket read: "Who chooses me shall find what everyone becomes in the end."

"I don't want that one," said the young man. "For not everyone becomes the husband of a duke's daughter."

The golden casket was opened, and it was full of dust and bones.

The silver casket said: "Who chooses me shall find what everyone gets in the end."

"No, take it away," ordered the youth. "For not everyone gets the daughter of a duke."

The silver casket was opened. Inside, it was full of moldy soil and wriggling worms.

The wooden casket had written on it: "Who chooses me finds what goodness grants."

"That's the one I want!" he declared. The wooden box was opened, and inside was a gorgeous golden ring set with diamonds and pearls.

"Well chosen," observed the duke's daughter, not without a little sigh. "Is that the prize worth having?"

"No," said the young man, "the prize is not this ring. The reward is to marry you – for is this not our engagement ring?"

"It is," the duke's daughter agreed – rather sadly. "You've solved the puzzle. We shall be married. Wear that ring always, for it is a token of the bond between us. Never part with it, or our wedding will not take place."

Proudly, the young man put the ring upon his finger. Then away he went to celebrate his success. With money left from his brother's loan, he bought food and wine. Soon his old friends were back and a grand time was had by all. By the time carnival had ended, all the money was spent.

With carnival over, the older brother sought the young man and demanded his money. His brother laughed and said, "I've nothing to pay you with today – all the money is gone. But wait just a little longer, for soon I'll be marrying the duke's daughter and will pay you ten times what I owe!"

"Scallywag! No daughter of a duke will marry you!" roared the brother. "Pay my money now, or I cut out a pound of your flesh this very day!"

The young man realized with horror that his brother was deadly serious. He pleaded for mercy, but the brother insisted on his pound of flesh. The youth was thrown into prison, so the matter could be judged.

"Let the duke solve this – I know he'll favor me!" boasted the older brother. "A bargain is a bargain, an agreement is an agreement, a contract is a contract, a deal is a deal. You signed the papers, you must pay with your flesh!"

Weeping and wailing, the younger brother paced his prison cell, thinking desperately about what he could do to save himself. Then an idea came to him. Hastily, he wrote a message and had the guard take it to the duke's daughter. She read it and came at once.

"Husband-to-be, how did you get thrown into my father's dungeons?" she asked. The young man told his story, of his recklessness with money and the conditions of the loan.

"This is bad, this is very bad," said the duke's daughter with a sigh. "You were foolish to put your life at risk, but it's also wicked for your brother to behave in this way. When you come to my father's court, you must have the best lawyer!"

"But lawyers cost money!" cried the young man. "And I have none."

"Never worry," smiled the duke's daughter. "I'll see to it you have a lawyer."

When the day came for the brothers to argue their case before the duke, his daughter dismissed all her servants. She cut off her hair and removed her beautiful gown of satin and lace. She put on instead the dusky robes of a lawyer. With short hair and dressed in these clothes, she passed easily for a man.

No one knew her as she entered the courtroom and declared herself to be the young man's advocate. The case was called, the brothers stepped forward.

The story was told to the duke, who looked over the documents and asked, "Is all this true?"

The young man admitted it was.

The duke frowned. "I don't like this case, this bad feeling between brothers. But it seems your brother has the right to cut away your flesh. Before I decide, what does the law say?"

The duke's daughter rose and proclaimed, "Your worship, the law says a bargain is a bargain, an agreement is an agreement, a contract is a contract, a deal is a deal. This young man borrowed the money, and can't pay it back. He agreed to give a pound of flesh instead, so his brother has the right to cut away that flesh this very instant."

The young man didn't much like the words of his lawyer. But then she went on, for lawyers do talk a lot.

"However," she said, "because a bargain is a bargain, an agreement is an agreement, a contract is a contract, a deal is a deal, it must be honored to the letter. The bargain was that exactly and precisely one pound of flesh be cut. So his brother must take no more and no less than a pound of flesh. If he cuts an ounce more or less than a pound, then he must give all his money to the city for breaking his word."

Now it was the older brother who was unhappy with the lawyer's words, but still the lawyer talked on.

"Furthermore," she declared, "the law says no person may spill the blood of another. If blood is spilled, then the older brother must have his head chopped off in punishment. So let exactly, precisely one pound of flesh be cut without a drop of blood spilled, or the older brother loses his money and his head. That is what the law says!"

"Excellent," cried the duke. "A brilliant reading of the law! You're the finest lawyer ever to speak in my court." Then he turned to the older brother: "Sir, take your pound of flesh without any blood, but break the law and you are ruined."

The older brother went away furious, with neither his money nor his pound of flesh. The younger brother was about to dash away to the duke's daughter to tell her the good news, when his lawyer stopped him.

"Sir, before you go, you must pay your lawyer," she declared.

"But I've no money," he croaked. "You know that. Just wait a little and my beloved will give me money to pay you."

"That won't do," said the duke's daughter, frowning. "You're a reckless young man, and I think not to be trusted. That ring on your finger – give it to me."

"I cannot!" the young man protested. "It was given to me by the duke's daughter. I promised never to remove it."

"Give it to me now," she commanded. "I shall hold it until you return with money to pay me."

Reluctantly, the young man gave her the ring. Then he dashed from the courtroom.

But the duke's daughter was quicker, and changed out of her clothes at once so he would not recognize her as his lawyer.

"My beloved, I'm saved!" he shouted as he raced up to her. "Now we can be married."

"That we cannot be," the duke's daughter calmly replied. "Look at your hand. Already you've lost the ring I made you promise to keep."

"But I had to pay the lawyer!" wailed the young man. "I had nothing else to give him."

"To pay a mere lawyer you gave up the prize worth having!" exclaimed the duke's daughter. "I think your love for me is too little. The bond between us is now broken – you'll not be my husband now!"

Both brothers were now disappointed in their fortunes. The younger one returned to the streets. A beggar once again, perhaps he was still happy-go-lucky, or maybe what had happened had made him wiser and more serious.

Meanwhile, the duke's daughter settled down happily with her books – pleased that she had saved two brothers from their wickedness and foolishness, but gladder still that it was she who had won a prize worth having.

·SNOWDROP·

As You Like It

Shakespeare wrote his play *As You Like It* at the end of the 1590s, basing it upon a book called *Rosalynde* by Thomas Lodge, written in about 1592. Following the plot of the book, the play tells of some young cousins whose family do not get along. One uncle is so evil, he takes over the dukedom from his brother, the rightful ruler. The rightful duke and his friends run away to the forest to live as outlaws, like Robin Hood and his Merry Men. His daughter, Rosalind, stays at court to keep her cousin company. Both girls fall in love – with brothers who fight like the father and uncle do in *Rosalynde*. When her uncle banishes her, Rosalind dresses as a boy and escapes with her cousin to live in the woods. There they join with the band of outlaws, who turn out to be old friends and relations. Soon all the lovers get together and the rightful duke is given back his dukedom.

Thomas Lodge based his book on a fourteenth-century poem called *The Tale of Gamelyn*, which has much in common with the legends of Robin Hood. In addition, it is possible that Lodge drew upon the fairy tale of "Snow White", also known as "Snowdrop", the oldest versions of which do not tell of her running off to live with the seven dwarves, but say rather that she joined a band of robbers. In all the stories, like the version retold here, the robbers are never wicked but more like Robin Hood and

ROSALIND

his Merry Men. Indeed, an English version of the story makes it clear that the robbers are related to the men of Sherwood Forest. Like Rosalind, the heroine often disguises herself in these stories, sometimes dressing as a man. Lodge set his story in France, and some of the oldest European versions of "Snow White/Snowdrop" come from that country, too. My retelling contains elements from various versions of "Snow White", including fairy tales from Turkey and a Scottish ballad which matches the *As You Like It* story particularly closely.

Like Lodge, Shakespeare set his story in France. But many people have noticed that the forest in *As You Like It* is more like a forest in England. In fact, it is like the forest that was once around Warwick Castle, near Shakespeare's boyhood home, Stratford-upon-Avon. Although he never wrote

a play about Robin Hood and his Merry Men, he mentions them in this play and says his characters are just like those ancient heroes.

In Shakespeare's time, plays about Robin Hood were very popular, as were romantic tales of country folk making merry in forests and carving love poetry on trees (in a similar way to Will in "Snowdrop"). The idea of a woman disguised as a man and living with outlaws was also highly popular – indeed, Shakespeare used the idea in two other plays, *Cymbeline* and *Twelfth Night*. So it may be that Shakespeare combined the fairy tale,

the old English legend of Robin Hood, and Lodge's book to create a play full of the things that audiences enjoy. Which is how the play gets its name – for it's written to be just as you (the audience) like it.

·SNOWDROP·

In a time before yours or mine, there was a queen who had a daughter. She called her Snowdrop, for the girl was as beautiful as the flowers of spring. The queen cared for Snowdrop more than anything in the world. Because of this, she neglected her duties and lost the kingdom to a man who was both clever and wicked. He banished the queen and made himself king, but he kept Snowdrop as a slave, to do all the work in the palace.

This new king was hard and cruel. His only joy was his son, a merry lad named Will. The king wished to raise his boy to be just like him.

But Will was not like his father, and cared nothing about ruling the kingdom. So, in spite of everything, Snowdrop and Will became the best of playmates and loved each other dearly.

The people in the kingdom were not happy with their harsh new ruler. They looked at Snowdrop and saw her goodness. They talked of how sweet and fair she was. They said the former princess should one day be their ruler, not Will, and certainly not his wicked father.

The king heard this and was furious. His hatred for Snowdrop grew until at last he couldn't bear the sight of her. In secret, the king ordered his most trusted servant to take Snowdrop to the forest and kill her.

Snowdrop overheard this plan, but she wasn't frightened. That night she packed a few things, kissed her playmate goodbye and ran into the forest to seek her own way in life.

She wandered around the forest until she was so tired and hungry she could go no farther. It was then that she stumbled upon a cave. Stepping inside, she found that the cave was like the finest palace, full of sparkling treasure.

"This is some robbers' den!" Snowdrop cried. "I've got to get out of here!"

Just as she was about to leave, she noticed a table in the middle of the cave – all laid out with the robbers' supper. The table was piled high with good things: cakes, pastries and all kinds of sweets!

Snowdrop was so famished she stopped to take a bite from each dish and a sip from each goblet. She made ready to leave once again, but it was too late. Clomp, clomp, came the sound of the robbers' feet. They were returning for their supper! Quick as a flash, Snowdrop jumped into a cupboard and closed the door behind her.

The three robbers, all brothers, saw at once someone had taken their food. Angrily they looked for this thief who had dared to rob them. Then the youngest discovered Snowdrop, shaking with fear in the cupboard.

"Brothers, I've found the thief! Not a bad catch, too!" he bragged.

"Grind his bones! Boil his blood! Mash his flesh!" ordered the older two robbers.

But when they saw Snowdrop, looking so sweet and gentle, they knew they couldn't harm her. Instead, they let her stay with them, promising to love and protect her as they would one another.

This was how Snowdrop became one of the robbers. She dressed as a man, and helped them in their work. They stole from the rich and used the money to help the weak and poor who suffered under the cruel king.

One day Snowdrop met up with her old playmate, Will. It came about this way.

Will was so lonely, he wandered into the woods each day, hoping to find Snowdrop. He even wrote poems in her honor, and hung them on every tree for her to find them. By following these love letters, Snowdrop finally tracked down Will.

Will didn't recognize her at first. When he did, he hugged her close and begged her to return with him to the palace. Snowdrop had to refuse.

"Please don't be sad," she said. "We've found each other again. And I'll see you every day – as long as you promise to stop writing those silly poems and hanging them on the trees! A robber can't have poetry written about her!"

Will promised. They met each day in a grove of apple trees and were wonderfully happy once again.

The king noticed his son's changed mood. He saw how happy Will was whenever he returned from the forest, and grew suspicious. So one day he followed his son to the apple grove, where he saw Will meeting Snowdrop. Seeing that the girl was still alive, his hatred grew stronger than ever and he resolved to get rid of Snowdrop once and for all.

Not long after that, the king disguised himself as a peddler woman. With a basket full of delights and dainties, he made his way into the forest, until he came to the robbers' cave. He knocked briskly upon the door of the cave, and Snowdrop answered.

"Good day, old woman," said Snowdrop. She did not recognize the king.

"Good day to you, my darling," croaked the wicked king. "Would you like to buy some trinkets from my basket?"

Now, the basket was full of baubles and laces and ribbons that caught the eye. One necklace shone brighter than all the rest, and it so pleased Snowdrop that she bought it at once. The king offered to fasten it around the girl's neck, pulling the necklace so tight it strangled Snowdrop and she fell to the ground. The evil king ran off, leaving her to die.

But Snowdrop's robber brothers returned to find her, and they loosened the necklace. They washed her hands and rubbed her face with vinegar and sugar water. Slowly the color came back to her cheeks, and she opened her eyes.

"Never, ever open that door when you're here alone!" the robbers made her promise.

Later, when the king followed Will to the apple grove, he saw his trick had been of no use. But his wickedness was such that he could not give up trying to destroy the girl. This time he made himself up as a flower seller and, with a basket of flowers, went back to the cave in the woods.

The king knocked, and talked sweetly, but Snowdrop wouldn't let him in, nor would she come out. So he left a bunch of poisoned flowers at the door, saying they were a gift to show he meant no harm. When the robbers returned, Snowdrop fetched the flowers and threw them straight on the fire. A terrible stink of poisonous fumes arose with the smoke.

"Never again," Snowdrop vowed, "do I speak to any old peddler women! I'm sure they've been sent by the king to destroy me."

The second old peddler woman – the king, that is – soon learned that Snowdrop still lived. He knew that Snowdrop and Will continued to meet and they loved each other more than ever.

So he filled a basket with magic poisoned apples and malignant pears. These he took to the grove where Will and Snowdrop met each day. He dropped the poisoned apples and pears all around that orchard. Then the king hid behind a tree, to be sure his plan worked and so he could see that Snowdrop was destroyed.

Soon Snowdrop came and waited for her friend. Seeing the apples lying on the ground, so pretty and red, she couldn't resist them. She picked up an apple, took one bite, and fell down dead.

With vicious glee, the king returned to the palace.

It was the robbers who found Snowdrop. They wept and cried, but this time they could not awaken her. So they fashioned a glass coffin for her to rest in. So beautiful was she, even in death, they could not bear to place her under the ground. Instead, they captured a wild horse and strapped the coffin to its back. They let the horse go – to wander through the land, carrying Snowdrop in her glass coffin so that all could gaze upon her beauty.

When Will came back to the apple grove, Snowdrop was not there. He waited but she did not come. Again his heart was broken from loneliness. He wandered for many days, looking for Snowdrop. Then, at last, he returned to the palace.

Word soon spread about the mysterious horse that carried a beautiful maiden, sleeping in a glass box. Many tried to catch a glimpse of this strange sight. Some feared it was a ghost. Others claimed it was fairy magic. But when the king heard the news, he only smiled, delighted that at last he had killed poor Snowdrop.

Then one day the wild horse wandered into the palace grounds. The guards, and all the lords and ladies of the court, stood back and gaped in amazement. They had heard of the strange vision, of the sleeping maiden in a glass coffin on a wild horse. But they had not believed it.

They were even more surprised when the king's son ran to the horse and grabbed hold of the coffin. Will had recognized his playmate. Weeping, he tried to loosen the coffin so as to take her from the horse and hold her in his arms.

The king saw that his son still loved the girl. In a rage, he dashed out and pushed the coffin from Will's hands. The glass case shattered upon the ground, and, as it fell, it so jolted Snowdrop that the piece of poisoned apple fell from her mouth. She awoke from death as though awakening from a long sleep.

Snowdrop told the astonished courtiers all that had happened since she had left the palace. The robbers were sent for, and they declared that Snowdrop had spoken truly.

Will ordered that the king be punished. The robbers placed magic shoes on the king's feet, and in these he danced and danced and could not stop dancing. He danced away, never to be seen again.

Meanwhile, Snowdrop and Will were married. Together, as queen and king, they ruled the land wisely and well. The banished queen returned to live with them in her old age. And the three robbers gave up their wild ways to live in the palace as Snowdrop's brothers, ready to offer help and advice whenever she needed it. As the youngest robber might have said, "And that was good, and it wasn't bad, was it?"

·ASHBOY·

Hamlet

Hamlet, written between 1599 and 1601, is Shakespeare's most famous play. It tells of a prince of Denmark, Hamlet, whose father has died. The father's ghost returns and informs his son that Hamlet's uncle poisoned him so that he could become king and marry Hamlet's mother. Hamlet is not sure if he can believe the ghost, or even be certain if the ghost is real. But he suspects something is truly wrong and hatches a plan to pretend he is mad, so as to find out if the ghost is right. When he learns all is true, he seeks revenge but dies fighting his uncle.

The play is based on a story from a history book written by the Danish historian Saxo Grammaticus about eight hundred years ago. He, in turn, based his book on an old Viking saga, which Shakespeare believed to be a true account. Old Norse sagas do portray real historic events, mixing them up with mystery and magic, and so it is possible that the story of Hamlet is partly true.

In the saga, the Hamlet character is a bit like the stepchild in fairy tales – Cinderella, for instance – who is badly treated by his or her family but, by sheer good luck, rises to become a king or queen. This character is

HAMLET

often given a name that suggests he is a fool or sleeps in the cinders by the fire. Hence, the boy in the tale retold here is named Ashboy.

In the original story, he is called Amlethi, a name that means "mad or crazy in battle", which suggests he seemed a bit stupid. The story retold here follows the saga, in which the boy is treated as a servant but acts as a "wise-fool" and succeeds in avenging his father's death by means of a few lucky encounters. In the play, however, Hamlet is no simpleton and only pretends to be mad. Shakespeare transformed the whole story, in fact, so that it is no longer about chance but about the difficult choices people must make in life.

Shakespeare may have decided to change the hero's name to Hamlet because in English it's easier to say than Amlethi. He may also have chosen it for personal reasons. His son Hamnet had died five years before, when he was only eleven years old. The same year that he wrote *Hamlet*, his own father died. Some people believe that when Shakespeare wrote the play he was thinking of his dead son and father.

The play is indeed about the sorrow a son feels for his dead father, but it is also about what goes wrong when people are bad or selfish. Many things seemed to be going wrong in England at that time. Harvests failed, people starved, prices rocketed, jobs were lost, and no one really believed that Elizabeth I and her government could solve these problems. Elizabeth was very old by then, with no one to take her place when she died, and so people worried, too, about what would happen after her death, and feared they might end up with a bad ruler.

·ASHBOY·

Long ago two kings ruled one land. They were brothers, and governed together. Horvendill and Feng they were called. Horvendill had a wife, Gertrood, and together they had a son.

Now everyone thought that the boy was a fool, an idiot. They really believed he was stupid. This was because he was always so quiet and still. His mother laughed at him and his uncle hated him. Only his father, Horvendill, loved the boy. Horvendill knew his son was the quiet type, who loved nothing more than to sit by the fire and watch and think about all he saw and heard.

Even so, "Ashboy, stupid Ashboy!" was what they all called him. He never complained about it – it only made him more shy – so the name stuck. Everyone forgot his real name, even his father.

Ashboy annoyed his uncle, just by existing. Feng's hatred of Ashboy grew so much that he began to hate his own brother as well. "It's all Horvendill's fault," grumbled Feng, "to have such a stupid boy who so annoys his uncle."

So Feng planned to kill Horvendill. With Gertrood's help, he would murder his brother.

One misty night, when the two brothers and Gertrood were out hunting, Feng shot his brother dead. Later he told everyone in the kingdom that they had become separated. He had tried to catch up with his brother, but had become lost in the fog.

Then, he said, he had heard Gertrood screaming. Thinking she was being attacked, he had run towards her and seen a strange shape in the fog, which he shot with his arrow. By mistake, he said, he had killed his own brother.

Feng seemed so upset that the people believed what he said. Shortly afterwards, Feng married Gertrood, saying that now that Horvendill was dead, he must take care of his wife. But quickly he declared that he and she were to be king and queen, to rule over all the land.

"No one knows the truth!" Feng and Gertrood said to themselves.

Only Ashboy knew what his uncle had done. He, too, had been out wandering that night for he liked the silence of the mist. He had witnessed all that had happened and knew that Feng had murdered Horvendill.

He saw how his mother happily forgot all about his father. He saw how his mother ignored him. Feng and Gertrood thought Ashboy was no bother to them. He was so stupid, he could never cause them any harm. That's what they thought.

But Ashboy just watched and waited. "I'll survive, and tell on them one day!" he swore. "I'll become a clown. No one will hate me then. When everyone likes me, they'll believe me when I tell the truth!"

He remained in the palace and entertained everyone. Every day he performed tricks. Ashboy juggled, he did somersaults and handstands, back flips and cartwheels. Whatever words he spoke were total nonsense. Everyone laughed and said, "What a joker!"

Cruel Feng thought it great fun to tease Ashboy. He would treat the boy as a prince, then make him look more stupid than he really was. Once, he invited the princess from a neighboring kingdom to his land. He introduced this lovely young woman to Ashboy and all the people. "This is Ashboy's wife!" he announced. "The two of them shall get married: the idiot clown and the beautiful princess."

Everyone laughed at that. It was a big joke. But Ashboy didn't laugh. Ashboy simply replied, "Uncle, I can't get married, for I've got no brother. If I'm murdered without a brother, who would my wife marry then?"

People guffawed even louder than before. They thought it was an even bigger joke than Feng's. But Feng and Gertrood didn't laugh. They realized Ashboy knew what had really happened. Suddenly the boy did not seem so stupid, and they feared him.

So Feng contrived to get rid of Ashboy. He called the boy in one day and said, "Ashboy, I'm sorry we made fun of you. Truly, I want you to marry the princess. You are a prince, not a clown. But everyone thinks you're a stupid fool. You must prove to them that you are a prince."

"How do I do that, Uncle?" asked Ashboy.

"Go with the princess to her land. Give this letter to her father," commanded Feng, handing him a sealed packet. "My neighbor, the king of that country, will read it and do as I say."

"But what did you write?" Ashboy begged to know.

"I have written to tell him that you must prove you are a hero," Feng replied. "I've asked the king to send you on adventures, to fight great battles. When you've done that, you can marry his daughter and become a real prince."

Ashboy took the letter and sailed away with the princess.

Neither knew what the letter truly said. Ashboy believed his uncle, which proves how innocent he was. But King Feng had lied. What he had really written was this:

Dear friend and neighbor, take the one who brings you this letter and kill him at once.

As luck would have it, Ashboy's ship got caught in a terrible storm. The ship sank, and only Ashboy and the princess survived. They managed to swim ashore, alive but exhausted. Ashboy fell into a deep sleep and the princess could not wake him. Hearing gruff voices coming towards them, she left Ashboy and ran to hide behind some rocks. She watched to see who the loud voices belonged to.

A band of big, ugly pirates had just landed from their ship. They saw Ashboy and thought he was a drowned man. "Search his pockets!" the pirate captain ordered. "We'll take any money we find. If he's still alive, slit his throat."

The brigands looked but found nothing on Ashboy except the letter from King Feng. This they tore open and their captain read it aloud. The pirates sighed. One felt so sorry for the boy that he cried.

"Poor lad," rumbled the cut throat. "A good-looking young fellow like that shouldn't be killed, especially by such a mean and nasty trick."

It was then the captain had a brilliant plan. Looking at the seal, the pirates could see that the letter was from one king to another. Because pirates don't like kings very much, they decided to play a trick themselves.

Carefully, the captain copied the letter, so that in every detail it looked like King Feng's writing. But when he had finished, the letter read:

Dear friend and neighbor, take the one who gives you this letter and marry him to your daughter the princess at once.

He carefully folded the new letter and slipped it into Ashboy's pocket. Roaring with laughter, the pirates left him sleeping and sailed away.

When Ashboy woke he had no idea of his good luck. But the princess, who had seen and heard all that had happened, came from her hiding place.

"Hurry," she ordered. "We must get to my father's palace as soon as we can."

Together they traveled to her father's palace and Ashboy delivered the letter. He thought the king would send him away at once. He would have great adventures and amazing exploits. He imagined that soon he'd fight giants and destroy dragons. But the only adventure he had was to get married. The king did just as the letter told him to do. Ashboy and the princess were wed at once.

That was a pretty big adventure. The princess was beautiful and he liked her very much.

Now the princess was wise and clever, but she could not let matters lie. She was as chatty and restless as Ashboy was quiet and thoughtful. And she was curious to know why Feng had written such a wicked letter. So she asked her husband, and Ashboy told her all he knew about his father's murder. In return she told Ashboy all she knew – about the pirates, and that his uncle wanted nothing more than to kill him, as he had King Horvendill.

Ashboy wept when he heard this. "What am I to do?" he cried.

The princess soothed him. "Don't worry, my love," she smiled. "I will help you."

Using her wisdom and wealth, her power and position, the princess raised a great army. She called for the finest ships to be built, the best men to be recruited. Together she and Ashboy sailed across the sea with this huge force.

They sailed to the land of King Feng and Queen Gertrood, and they made war. There was banging and blasting and all kinds of bombardment. There was stabbing and slashing. There was great slaughter altogether. The war was so fiercely fought that the green grass turned red with blood and the blue sky turned black with smoke.

But in the end, Ashboy destroyed King Feng. And the princess locked Queen Gertrood in a deep dark dungeon, full of toads and spiders and slimy snakes.

Ashboy and the princess were crowned king and queen of that land. And if they didn't settle down comfortably, the two of them certainly lived lives of great excitement and wild adventure. But all that's a different story, to be told another time…

·CAP-O-RUSHES·

King Lear

King Lear, written 1604–5, is a play about a king with three daughters. He is old, and decides to retire and leave the kingdom to be run by his children and their husbands. But the youngest daughter, Cordelia, makes him angry and he sends her away. Then he discovers that the other two daughters want only his power and money, and do not wish to take care of him in his old age. They chase him away, and, accompanied only by his court jester, he goes slowly mad. Cordelia returns with her new husband and an army to fight the armies of her sisters and their husbands. The selfish daughters lose the war, but by the time King Lear and Cordelia find each other again, it is too late, for they die soon afterwards.

This play has its roots in one of the oldest, best-loved folk tales, known thoughout the world. It goes by various names, including "More than Salt", "As Much as Salt" and "Cap-O-Rushes". This last version was the one I was told as a child, and I tell it almost exactly as I first heard it long ago. All versions of the folk tale begin in the same way as the play, with the king asking his daughters how much they love him. While the play

KING LEAR.

How sharper than a serpent's tooth it is

then goes on to tell what happened to the father, the folk tale follows the fate of the youngest daughter after she has been banished. In most versions of the story, her adventures are like those of Cinderella and other well-known fairy-tale heroines. "Cinderella" and "Cap-O-Rushes" probably come from the same ancient story, created thousands of years ago.

Some say Shakespeare got his idea for the play after reading a version of this story in a history book, the *Chronicles*, written by Holinshed in 1577. The historical account has a happy ending, for Cordelia doesn't die but survives to become Queen of Britain. Her capital is believed by some people to have been in the middle of England, where the city of Leicester is today. In fact, that's how Leicester got its name, for it means "the fortress of Lear".

In both the play and the story, King Lear asks his children how much they love him. As a result of this question, the king and his daughters learn the true meaning of love and that people in the same family can cause each other both happiness and pain. When Shakespeare wrote *King Lear*, his daughters, Susanna and Judith, were in their early twenties and late teens – old enough to get married and leave home. Perhaps Shakespeare had his own daughters in mind, and his own mixed feelings about them growing up and leaving him, when he wrote the play.

It is possible that he also had in mind an event that had taken place not long before he wrote the play. This concerned a wealthy Londoner whose two older daughters tried to make people think the old man was insane so they could get his riches. But his youngest daughter defended her father, and so proved her love to be true – just like Cordelia in the play or Cap-O-Rushes in the folk tale.

CORDELIA

·CAP-O-RUSHES·

Once upon a time there was a king. Everyone thought he was wise and good. Yet once he asked a foolish question and suffered sorely as a result. The king had three daughters, princesses who were beautiful, good and wise. He wanted to test them.

When he had the three before him, he asked, "Children, how much do you love me?"

The first said, "Father, I love you as much as all the gold and silver in the world."

The second said, "Father, I love you as much as all the gems and jewels in the earth."

These two answers pleased the king. But the third princess was the most sensible and always answered honestly. She spoke simply, and did not flatter or tease.

The third princess said, "Father, I love you as much as salt."

The king flew into a rage. "That means you love me not at all. Everyone has salt. You stupid goose, you don't love me enough. From this day on you are banished."

The princess tried to explain. She tried to make her father understand and change his mind. But he wouldn't listen. So the princess left the home she had always known. Without servants or soldiers, nor a horse to carry her, she set off to seek her fortune. All she took were three dresses that had once belonged to her dead mother, the queen.

When at last the princess arrived in a land where no one knew her, she hid the three dresses in a hollow tree in the forest. Then she bathed in the river and made a skirt, a cape and a cap out of the long green rushes that grew at the edge of the water. Dressed like this, she started looking for work. She had to make her way in the world.

The princess went to the castle belonging to the prince of that foreign land. She asked the cook for a job. He didn't like the look of her and said no. But she begged and begged, and finally he relented.

"You can stay to scrub the pots and pans," he sniffed. "All you'll get for it is a place by the fire to sleep, and the scraps of food we don't want."

So it was that the princess found a living scraping pots and pans. In return she was given a place in the ashes to sleep, and the tidbits the servants didn't want, they threw to her to eat. Because she wore a dress and hat made of rushes, they called her Cap-O-Rushes. Cap-O-Rushes worked in the castle kitchens for a long time.

One day the prince of that land announced he would hold a festival, to last three days and three nights. Everyone was invited, rich and poor alike. The servants said the prince was going to choose a wife at the festival. Each serving maid thought he might pick her.

But on the first day of the festival, Cap-O-Rushes said she was too tired to go. The servants left her asleep by the fire. Once she was alone, she ran to the forest and bathed in the river. Cap-O-Rushes put on the first dress that had belonged to her mother. This was a gown made of gold. When she wore it, she shone like the sun in the sky. That is how she went to the festival.

When she entered the great hall where people were feasting and making merry, everyone stopped to stare. They had never seen such beauty. Spellbound, the prince went up to her and asked her for every dance. Yet Cap-O-Rushes would not tell him her name, nor from where she came. Before the first day of the festival was over, she was gone. Nobody knew where.

When the servants returned to the kitchens, they found Cap-O-Rushes asleep in her old clothes. No one knew she had been the radiant princess dressed in gold.

On the second day, Cap-O-Rushes was again left alone, sleeping in the ashes. At once she ran to the forest and washed in the river. Dressed in her mother's second gown, which was made of silver, she looked like the glistening moon, skipping and tripping above the clouds.

Just as before, she was the most beautiful woman at the festival. The prince danced only with her. Yet he could not learn her name, nor find out where she lived. Before the day was over, she was gone again. The servants found Cap-O-Rushes sleeping by the fire. They still did not recognize her as the shimmering princess.

The last day of the festival the servants could not rouse Cap-O-Rushes from her slumber. When she was alone, she ran to the forest and dressed in the third gown, made of gems and jewels. Wearing that dress, Cap-O-Rushes glittered like the stars. As soon as she arrived, the prince took her by the hand and would not let her go.

"Won't you tell me your name at least?" he implored. But Cap-O-Rushes would not. So the prince took a ring from his finger and put it on Cap-O-Rushes' hand.

"By the ring I will find you and know you, and with this ring I will marry you," he promised.

Cap-O-Rushes just smiled. Still she said nothing. She was worried about how she might escape. On this, the final day of the festival, the prince held tightly to her hand and would not let go for an instant. She feared he would discover she was a kitchen maid, and there would be trouble. But then there was a dance where everyone changed partners. The prince had to let go, and, free at last, Cap-O-Rushes made a dash for the kitchens. She was in her old clothes, asleep, when the other servants returned.

The next day the prince began to search for the woman to whom he had given the ring. But he looked only at grand women – all done up in their finest clothes. He looked at princesses, countesses and duchesses. Never once did he consider ordinary women who worked for a living. So he did not find Cap-O-Rushes.

The prince returned and took to his bed. The doctors announced that he had a broken heart and would die for love. Everyone said that was a shame – everyone, that is, but Cap-O-Rushes. When she heard the news, she just laughed out loud.

The cook said she was wicked to laugh about the prince dying.

"But that's not why I laugh," said the girl. "I laugh because the prince will not die. I could make some soup that will cure him."

"Well then," snorted the cook, "you'd better do it!"

And she did. When the soup was made, and no one was looking, Cap-O-Rushes put the prince's ring into the dish. It was taken to the prince, who drank it. There at the bottom of the bowl he found the ring.

"Whoever made the soup must come at once!" he commanded, immediately feeling much better.

The cook feared something must have been wrong with the soup and didn't want Cap-O-Rushes to take the blame for it. He was fond of her and didn't want her to get into trouble. So he went to the prince.

"Who made the soup?" inquired the young man.

"I did, Your Highness," smiled the cook, and bowed deeply.

The cook was a short, fat, balding old man. "Oh no, you can't have made the soup," said the prince. "Send the one who did – I promise no harm will come to her."

The kindly cook went to Cap-O-Rushes and sent her to the prince, saying, "It's no good – he wants you and he's going to get you!"

When Cap-O-Rushes entered the prince's chamber, he asked, "How came you by the ring?"

She looked him in the eye and said, "By him who gave it to me."

Now from the moment she entered the room, the prince knew she was the one to whom he had given the ring. When she saw that he recognized her, Cap-O-Rushes removed her skirt, cape and cap of rushes, showing beneath it her gown of gems and jewels.

As he had promised he asked, "Princess, will you marry me and be my queen?"

And she agreed.

They planned a big wedding. They even invited her father, the wise old king who had asked the foolish question. When Cap-O-Rushes heard he was coming to the wedding, not knowing it was his own daughter's, she told the cook, "Make the food for my wedding with no salt. Not a handful of salt, not a pinch of salt, not a grain of salt. No salt at all, in fish or flesh or fowl, in pudding or pie or pastry, in soup or broth, in fruit or vegetable. No salt at all!"

"That'll taste nasty!" complained the cook.

"It doesn't matter – just do as I say," Cap-O-Rushes ordered.

So the food for the wedding was made without salt. When the guests sat down at the wedding banquet, the food tasted terrible. They all complained, saying, "The wedding is ruined, there's no salt in the food!"

All complained except Cap-O-Rushes' father. The wise old king began to cry. He wept so much that his long white beard was soaked with tears.

The guests all asked, "Why are you crying?"

The old king replied, "Once I had a daughter and I asked how much she loved me. She said she loved me as much as salt, and I thought that meant she did not love me at all. But now I understand. Without salt, food has no taste. Without love, life has no meaning. My daughter loved me more than all the world, and I've lost her forever!"

Again he wept. Cap-O-Rushes could bear it no longer. She ran up to her father and put her arms around him. Kissing him tenderly, she said, "Ah, no, dearest father, you've not lost your daughter. Because I am she and I love you still."

The king looked into her eyes and recognized the child he had sent away. He begged her forgiveness, and, of course, she forgave him. Then she ordered the cook to make fresh food, but this time with salt. The cook went off at once to prepare a new banquet for the guests.

The wedding of Cap-O-Rushes and the prince was such a grand party, such a glorious affair, that it lasted seven years and a day. Each day was better than the one before. And how do I know this? I was at the wedding myself, and that's how I heard the story.

ANTIGONUS: "Come, poor babe,
I have heard but not believed,

THE·FLOWER·PRINCESS

The Winter's Tale

The Winter's Tale, written in about 1610 or 1611, is one of Shakespeare's last plays. It tells of the King of Sicily, who is so jealous of his wife that he suspects his best friend, the King of Bohemia, is in love with her. He fights with his friend and when a daughter is born, insists that he himself is not the child's father. The queen appears to die of shame, while a faithful servant rescues the baby and takes her away to Bohemia. Here the child is raised by a poor shepherd and named Perdita, which means "lost one". The King of Bohemia's son falls in love with Perdita. This angers his father, who thinks she is not good enough to marry his boy. The young lovers run away to the land of Perdita's father, the jealous king. He regrets what he has done and when the full story is revealed, everyone is reunited and Perdita's mother appears again – not dead, but disguised as a statue which comes to life.

The play is based on a popular book, *Pandosto or The Triumph of Time*, written in 1588 by Robert Greene. Woven into Greene's story are elements of fairy tales from many different countries. In the book and many of the folk tales related to it, the action starts in Bohemia and then moves to Sicily. Shakespeare changed the setting around. No one is quite sure why, but one thing is certain: it shows that he was not very good at geography, for in his play the banished princess is washed up on the

LEONTES

If such a thing be,
thy mother appear'd to me last night,

KING JAMES I of England

shores of Bohemia. Bohemia is now the Czech Republic, and doesn't touch the sea!

The story retold here follows Shakespeare's setting but is otherwise based on Greene's book and various ballads, including *The Royal Courtly Garland*, or *Joy After Sorrow*, which is strikingly similar to *The Winter's Tale*. Another source is "The Gardener Prince", an old English fairy tale which is believed to come from Bohemia and which could have been one of the tales used by Greene for his book.

One reason Greene's novel was popular in the early 1600s was because the story (which includes a king and his son disagreeing about who the prince should marry) matched the gossip about the new king of England, James I, who was arguing with his son, Prince Henry, about the same problem. Shakespeare's company of players knew that if they presented this book as a play, many people would come to see it.

But that is probably not the only reason Shakespeare decided to adapt the book as a play. Almost all his last plays are about fathers and daughters. Shakespeare's elder daughter, Susanna, had married a Puritan and, as Puritans disapproved of the theater, it is possible that he and Shakespeare didn't always get along. Meanwhile, his younger daughter, Judith, was being courted by a man who proved to be untrustworthy. At the same time, the only grandchild Shakespeare knew while he was alive was born. With all these family joys and sorrows, maybe it was only natural for Shakespeare to find and retell stories about fathers and daughters and their problems.

PERDITA

THE·FLOWER·PRINCESS

There was once a young King of Sicilia who was selfish, restless and hard-hearted. His people wished he would fall in love and settle down. But the king said this would never happen.

Yet one day the king met a young country girl. "You're so beautiful!" he exclaimed.

That she was, and as kind and generous as the king was mean-spirited. His heart softened and he fell in love with her. Before long, the king asked her to be his wife.

The two were married. The new queen was so good that the king changed his ways. He followed her example, and became more like her. People were delighted. "How gentle and kind the king is when he wants to be!" they observed.

After a time, the queen gave birth to a little girl. Everyone rejoiced. The wisest wise woman in the world was invited to the celebrations. She was the queen's best friend, and an oracle – she could foretell the future. On the day the princess was named, many people presented gifts. But the finest came from the wise woman. She gave the little girl a golden chain with a pendant in the shape of a flower.

The old woman revealed, "She'll be called Flora, for her joys and sorrows will be among the flowers. Those joys and sorrows will be shared by all who love her."

The King of Sicilia didn't like the sound of this. His daughter was a princess, not a wild girl who roamed among the flowers of the fields and forests. From that time on, he cared nothing for his child.

But the Queen of Sicilia doted on the little girl. The princess got all her attention. The king resented this. He returned to his mean ways and finally shouted at the queen, "You act like a stupid country woman, fussing over your baby so! We have servants to do that!"

Amazed at her husband's words, the queen quietly replied, "I am a country woman, and proud of it. And you knew that when you married me. But country woman or queen, I shall always take care of my child and never leave my girl to fend for herself."

"You will!" roared the king. "Let the princess be left alone, without mother or servants."

In a rage, the King of Sicilia ordered that the child be placed in her cradle, and that the cradle be dropped into the river that ran beside the palace. The order was carried out at once.

Horrified at what her husband had done, the queen fled to the highest tower and locked herself in. Weeping and wailing, she would see no one except the wise woman who had foretold joy and sorrow for her baby, though it seemed the baby's fate was to be all sadness.

"Please let me see you!" the king implored.

No matter how the king begged, his wife wouldn't allow him into the tower. After many days, the wise woman reported, "The queen has died of a broken heart."

The king heard this and fell into a faint. When he awoke, he tore his clothes and covered himself in ashes. Moaning and weeping, he would not be comforted. From that time on, he mourned the loss of his daughter and the death of his wife, all caused by his own pride and anger.

In the meantime, the cradle didn't sink, but floated down the river and across the sea. At last, it was washed up on the shores of Bohemia, a land far from Sicilia. The cradle tipped the princess onto the sand, and it was there an old man found her.

The old fellow could not think where the child had come from, nor how she had come to be there. There had been no storms, no shipwrecks at all. Even so, he took her home. The old man and his wife had always wished for a child and none had been born to them. "The child is a blessing on us," he decided. "This little girl is the answer to our prayers."

His wife smiled. "Her name's Flora," she announced, "for she wears a golden flower on the chain around her neck."

They raised Flora as their own child. Because the two were gardeners, and tended the gardens of the King of Bohemia, Flora became a gardener, too. She dwelled among flowers every day. Her foster parents were kind and good. So far, the prophecy had proved to be true: starting life in sorrow, Flora now knew great joy.

Flora grew to be as beautiful and good as her mother, the queen, once had been. Bruno, the Prince of Bohemia, saw her at work in the gardens, and he fell in love with her. Every day as he strolled through the palace grounds, he would steal a glance at her. His father did not like this.

"From now on, keep out of the gardens," the King of Bohemia ordered him, like a typical bossy father. "Remain in the palace and stay away from that horrible girl!"

But Bruno disobeyed his father. One day he went to the gardens. When he saw Flora, he wanted more than anything to give her a present, even though he had never once had the nerve to talk to her. So he reached towards a bush to pick a rose.

"Stop!" Flora warned. "Don't touch any flowers on that bush. It's magic!"

Bruno didn't listen, and Flora's warning came too late. As he grasped a rose, a thorn pricked his hand. The prince fell to the ground in a deep sleep.

Flora cried for help and servants carried Bruno to his bed. Doctors were sent for, yet all their pills and potions couldn't cure the careless young man. Prince Bruno slept on and on.

At last, the King of Bohemia was so desperate, he sent for the wisest wise woman in the world. She was the oracle who had given Flora the golden chain. The old woman declared, "The only cure for Bruno is that he be kissed by Flora and the two get married at once."

The king didn't like that at all. He wanted his son to be cured, but he did not want the prince to have a mere gardener for a wife. So he plotted and planned. Flora was called, and told to kiss the prince. She happily did so. As soon as their lips touched, Bruno opened his eyes to look around. He was delighted to see Flora.

But the king was ready. "Seize Flora and throw her into the sea!" he cried.

The command was carried out instantly, and Flora was tossed into the sea.

Whether it was because of the direction of the current, or the ebb and flow of the tide, or whether it was the magic of the wisest wise woman, it can't be said. But however it came about, Flora floated across the sea and back to the land of Sicilia, the land of her true father and mother.

She was met by the wisest wise woman, who took her at once to the tower where her mother, the queen, had once hidden. Now it was Flora who hid there.

Meanwhile, Bruno's heart was filled with sadness and anger. He screamed at his father, "How could you destroy the only girl I loved? I'll never live in this land, or look at you again until I find her!"

So he set off in search of Flora. For a long time he traveled, until at last the winds brought him to Sicilia, that sad, sorry place which was Flora's real home. He arrived at the king's palace. Here the King of Sicilia, after all these years, still ruled. All that time he had sat, miserable and lonely, upon his throne. His clothes were torn and ragged. Ashes and dust covered his body. A pool of tears caused by years of weeping drenched his feet.

His moaning and groaning were echoed by the constant sighing of the lovelorn prince.

"Young man," observed the king, "you seem as sad as me. Tell me why."

Bruno told his story, and of his search for Flora. Then the King of Sicilia told of his foolishness and anger, and how, through them, he had lost both wife and child. The two men wept until the growing pool of tears threatened to drown everyone in the palace.

Then it was that the wisest wise woman appeared. "You stupid idiots!" she cried in exasperation. "Go to the tower immediately. And for once in your lives, use your brains! Don't speak and don't act before you think."

Amazed, the two men climbed the tower that had for so long been locked. At the top of the tower they found the most wonderful painting. The picture showed two women of great beauty. To the king, the older one looked just like his wife, the Queen of Sicilia. To Bruno, the younger one appeared to be Flora, but in the clothes of a princess, not of a gardener, and still with the flower pendant around her neck.

So shocked were they that the two men did not need to remember to think before they spoke or acted. Instead, they stood like statues. They thought how nothing could have surprised them more than this painting.

But then something even more amazing happened – the painting came to life! The two women in the picture began to move and to sing a song so merry that it dried the men's tears and they laughed more than they had ever done in all their lives.

Then the queen and Flora stepped out of the painting, and ran to put their arms around their loved ones. In all those years, the queen had not been dead but living secretly in the tower, protected by the magic of the oracle. The wise woman had returned Flora to her mother as soon as the princess' feet had touched her native land.

All these stories were told, all the sorrows and joys recounted. Then Bruno married Flora, and they lived in joy and sorrow – but mostly in joy – from that time onwards.

·SOURCES·

Writing this book was a bit like going on a treasure hunt. I knew some of the stories already – they had been told to me when I was young, by my family and teachers. Others I learned as I grew up and became friends with older storytellers who shared their repertoire of tales with me. But I wanted to find out where the stories came from, and what they were like in Shakespeare's day. So I looked up stories in old books. I visited libraries and hunted for as many storybooks and ballad collections as possible. I looked at some of the original books, printed in Shakespeare's own time. I also looked up lots of books about Shakespeare himself, and what life in England was like in his day.

Each of Shakespeare's plays seems to be related to old stories that have many, many different versions. So I've tried to find all those variants and pick and mix the bits I like best, telling them in a way that I hope you'll like. This is what storytellers, including Shakespeare, have always done with these stories.

Below are listed some of the books that helped me retell the tales in this book. You will find some in your local public library. Many can only be found in special libraries, like The British Library, the Guildhall Library, the Folklore Society Library and the Vaughan Williams Memorial Library – all in London.

GENERAL SOURCES FOR ALL THE STORIES

Aarne, Antti, *The Types of Folktale: A Classification and Bibliography*, translated and enlarged by Stith Thompson, Suomalainen Tiedeakatemia, Helsinki, and Indiana Unversity Press, Bloomington, 1961.
Booth, Stephen, *A Book Called Holinshed's Chronicles*, Book Club of California, San Francisco, 1968.
Brand, John, *Popular Antiquities of Great Britain*, Reeves and Turner, London, 1905.
Bullough, Geoffrey (ed.), *Narrative and Dramatic Sources of Shakespeare*, 8 vols, Routledge & Kegan Paul, London, and Columbia University Press, New York, 1957–75.
Collier, John Payne, *Shakespeare's Library: A Collection of the Romances, Novels, Poems and Histories Used by Shakespeare as the Foundation of his Dramas, with Introductions by W. C. Hazlitt*, Thomas Rudd, London, 1850; Reeves and Turner, London, 1875.
Davis, Madison J., and Frankforter, A. Daniel, *The Shakespeare Name and Place Dictionary*, Fitzroy Dearborn Publishers, London and Chicago, 1995.
Eastman, Mary Huse (ed.), *The Index to Fairy Tales, Myths, and Legends*, F. W. Faxon Co., Boston, 1926.
 Supplement to the Index of Fairy Tales, Myths, and Legends and *Second Supplement to the Index of Fairy Tales, Myths, and Legends*, F. W. Faxon Co., Boston, 1937 and 1952.
Gesta Romanorum, 1340; first printed in English by Wynkeyn de Worde in the early 1500s and by Richard Robinson in 1648.
Gesta Romanorum, or Entertaining Moral Stories, translated by the Reverend Charles Swan, London, 1824.
Hazlitt, William Carew, *English Drama & Stage Under the Tudor and Stuart Princes*, 1543–1664, Chiswick Press, London, 1869.
 English Proverbs and Proverbial Phrases, Chiswick Press, London, 1869; Gale Research Co., Detroit, 1969.
 Fairy Tales, Legends and Romances Illustrating Shakespeare and Other English Writers, Frank and William Kerslake, London, 1875.
 Jests, New & Old, J. W. Jarvis & Son, London, 1887.
 Shakespeare's Jest-Books: Re-prints of Early and Rare Jest-Books Supposed to Have Been Used by Shakespeare, Willis & Sotheran, London, 1864.
 Tales and Legends of National Origin, or Widely Current in England, Sonnenschein & Company, London, 1892.
Haworth, Peter, *An Elizabethan Story-Book, Famous Tales from the Palace of Pleasure*, Longman, Green and Company, London, 1928.
Holinshed, Raphael, *The Firste Volume of the Chronicles of England, Scotlande and Irelande* and *The Last Volume of the Chronicles of England, Scotlande, and Irelande*, 1577 and 1587.
Painter, William, *Palace of Pleasure*, 1566.
Rushton, William Lowes, *Shakespeare Illustrated*, 2 vols, Shepman, London, 1867 and 1868.
Thomson, Stith, *Motif Index of Folk Literature*, Rosenkilde & Bagger, Copenhagen, and Indiana University Press, Bloomington, 1955.

GENERAL SOURCES FOR INFORMATION ABOUT SHAKESPEARE'S LIFE AND ELIZABETHAN/JACOBEAN TIMES

Aydelotte, Frank, *Elizabethan Rogues and Vagabonds*, Clarendon Press, Oxford, 1913; Frank Cass & Co., London, 1967.
Brinkworth, C. R. C., *Shakespeare and the Bawdy Court of Stratford*, Phillimore & Co., London and Chichester, 1972.
Chambers, E. K., *The English Folk Play*, Clarendon Press, Oxford, 1933.
 English Literature at the Close of the Middle Ages, Clarendon Press, Oxford, 1945.
 English Pastorals, Blackie & Sons, London, 1895.
 The Elizabethan Stage, 4 vols, Clarendon Press, Oxford, 1923.
 The Medieval Stage, 2 vols, Clarendon Press, Oxford, 1903.
 Notes on the History of the Revels Office under the Tudors, A. H. Bullen, London, 1906.
 The Oxford Book of Sixteenth Century Verse, Clarendon Press, Oxford, 1932.
 Shakespeare Gleanings, Oxford University Press, Oxford, 1944.

Shakespeare: A Survey, Sidgwick & Jackson, London, 1925.
Sir Thomas Wyatt and Some Collected Studies, Sidgwick & Jackson, London, 1933.
The Stage of the Globe, Clarendon Press, Oxford, 1907.
William Shakespeare: A Study of Facts and Problems, Clarendon Press, Oxford, 1930.
Greer, Germaine, *Shakespeare*, Past Masters, Oxford University Press, 1986.
Hardy, Barbara, *Shakespeare's Storytellers*, Peter Owen, London, 1997.
Lee, Sir Sidney, *Great Englishmen of the Sixteenth Century*, Archibald Constable & Co., London, 1904.
Meads, Chris, *Elizabethan Humour*, Robert Hale, London, 1995.
Muir, Kenneth, "Folklore and Shakespeare", *Folklore*, 92:11, 1981.
Thomson, Peter, *Shakespeare's Professional Career*, Cambridge University Press, Cambridge, 1992.
Wadleigh Chandler, Frank, *The Literature of Roguery*, 2 vols, Archibald Constable & Co., London, and Houghton, Mifflin & Co.,
    Boston, 1907.
Wright, Louis B., *Middle-Class Culture in Elizabethan England*, University of North Carolina Press, Chapel Hill, 1935.
Wright, William Aldis (ed.), *The Complete Works of William Shakespeare*, Doubleday & Co., New York, 1936.
Zesmer, David M., *Guide to Shakespeare*, Barnes & Noble Books, New York, 1976.

SOURCES FOR THE STORIES

THE DEVIL'S BET

Afanas'ev, A. N., "The Taming of the Shrew", *Russian Fairy Tales*, translated by Norbert Guterman, George Routledge & Sons,
    London, 1946.
Bay, J. C., "Bend the Bough in Time", *Danish Folk and Fairy Tales*, Harper and Bros., New York and London, 1899.
Bord, Janet and Colin, *The Enchanted Land: Myths and Legends of Britain's Landscape*, Thorsons, London, 1995.
Briggs, Katharine, "The Watchers at the Well", *A Dictionary of British Folk Tales*, 4 vols, Routledge & Kegan Paul, London, part A,
    vol. 1, 1970.
Edwards, Richard, *The Waking Man's Dream*, sixteenth century.
Grimm, J. and W., "King Thrushbeard", *The Complete Grimms' Fairy Tales*, Pantheon Books, New York, 1944.
Kennedy, Patrick, "The Haughty Princess", *The Fireside Stories of Ireland*, McGlashon & Gill, Dublin and London, 1870.
    Legendary Fiction of the Celts, Macmillan, London, 1866.
OhOgain, Daithi, "The Bet, or The Taming of the Shrew", unpublished manuscript, transcript of a field recording in Wicklow
    Mountains in the 1970s.
Sayers, Peig (1873-1958), collected by Kenneth Jackson from her on the Great Blasket, County Kerry, in the period 1932-37,
    entitled *An Cailn Ceann-Dine*, republished as *Scaltan mBlascaod* (Dublin, 1938 pp. 23-25) in *Baloideas*, the Journal of the
    Folklore of Ireland Society, edited by Seamus Duilearga, M.A., published for the Society by The Educational Company of
    Ireland, Dublin, 1938.

THE HILL OF ROSES

Brooke, Arthur, *The Tragicall History of Romeus & Juliet*, 1562.
Garter, Bernard, *The Tragicall & True Historie which Happened between Two English Lovers*, 1563.
MacPherson, George W., "The Stone of Roses", *Traditional Stories of Northwest Skye*, Skye Graphics, Skye, 1984.
Masuccio, Salernitano, *Il Novellino*, 1474.
    The Thirty-third Novel of Il Novellino, translated by Maurice Jones, Davis and Oriolli, London, 1917.
    The Novellino of Masuccio, 2 vols, translated by W. G. Waters, Lawrence & Bullen, London, 1895.
Painter, William, "The Goodly Hystory of the Love between Rhomeo and Julietta", *Palace of Pleasure*, 1566; also featured in
    Collier's *Shakespeare's Library* (see General Sources).
Porta, Luigi da, *Istoria novellamente ritrovata di due nobili amanti*, 1535; translated into English by Sir Geoffrey Fenton, 1567.
Xenophon of Ephesus, "The love-adventure of Abrocomas and Anthia", *Ephesiaca (The Ephesian Story)*, translated by Paul Turner,
    Golden Cockerel Press, London, 1957.

A BARGAIN IS A BARGAIN

Brewer, E. C., *A Dictionary of Miracles, Imitative, Realistic, and Dogmatic, with Illustrations*, Chatto & Windus, London, 1884.
Conway, Moncure David, *The Wandering Jew*, Chatto & Windus, London, 1991.
    "Dolopathos and the Seven Wise Men", story originating in the eleventh–thirteenth centuries. The oldest written version
    (in Latin) is *Dolopathos, sive opusculum de rege et septum sapientibus* by Johannes de Alta Silva, Haute Seille, France, 1207–12.
        There are also versions in French by Herbers "le clerc" and Trouvère (the minstrel), written down in the mid–late thirteenth
        and early fourteenth centuries.
Fiorentino, Giovanni, *Il Pecorone*, a collection of tales published circa 1378.
    The Novel from which the Play of the Merchant of Venice, written by Shakespeare, is taken, translated by M. Cooper, 1755.
    The Pecorone of Ser Giovanni, translated by W. G. Waters, Lawrence & Bullen, London, 1897.
Friedlander, Gerald, *Shakespeare and the Jew*, George Routledge & Sons, London, 1921.
Furnace, Horace Howard (ed.), *The New Variorum Edition of Shakespeare*, J. B. Lippincott Co., Philadelphia and London, 1890.
Gladwin, F., *The Persian Moonshee*, Calcutta, 1795, and London, 1801.
Leti, Gregorio, *Vita di Sisto V*, 1686; printed in English by John Wyatt as *The Biography of Pope Sixtus V*, 1704.
Mahabharata, 200 BC–AD 200, source for an early "bond of flesh" tale, often called the "Dove and the Hawk" story.
Silvayn, Alex, "Of A Jew Who Would for his Debt Have a Pound of Flesh of a Christian", *Orator*, translated by A. Munday, 1598.
"The Story of the Choice of Three Caskets", *Gesta Romanorum* (see General Sources).

SNOWDROP

Briggs, Katharine, "Snow White", *A Dictionary of British Folk Tales*, 4 vols, Routledge & Kegan Paul, London, part A, vol. 1, 1970.

Child, Francis James (ed.), "Rose the Red and Lillie the White", *English and Scottish Ballads*, 8 vols, Little, Brown & Company, and Shepard, Clark and Brown, Boston, vol. 5, 1859.

Garnett, L. M. J. (trans.), "Queen of the Night", *Ottoman Wonder Tales*, A. & C. Black, London, 1915.

Kúnos, Dr Ignácz (trans.), "The Magic Hair Pins", *Forty-four Turkish Fairy Tales*, George Harrap & Company, London, 1913.

Lodge, Thomas, *Rosalynde*, 1592.
   The Complete Works of Thomas Lodge, 1580–1623, 4 vols, Hunterian Club, Glasgow, 1883.

Philip, Neil (ed.), "Snow White", English Fairy Tales, Penguin Books, Harmondsworth, 1992.

ASHBOY

Morley, Henry, *Early Prose Romances*, George Routledge & Sons, London, 1889.

Saxo Grammaticus, *Gesta Danorum*, thirteenth century.
   The First Nine Books of the Danish History of Saxo Grammaticus, translated by Oliver Elton, David Nutt, London, 1894.

Thoms, William J., *Early English Prose Poems. Revised and enlarged, including a reprint of Morley's Early Prose Romances*, George Routledge & Sons, London, and E. P. Dutton & Co., New York, 1907.

CAP-O-RUSHES

Ashe, Geoffrey, *Mythology of the British Isles*, Methuen, London, 1990.

Dougherty, Katherine and Ellen: unpublished transcript of the "Cap-O-Rushes" story collected from my great-aunts.

Folklore Myths and Legends of Britain, Reader's Digest Association, London, 1973.

Geoffrey of Monmouth (also known as Monumetensis Galfridus, Bishop of St Asaph), *Historia Regum Britanniae*, circa 1136.
   (under the name Galfridus), *Regum Britanni carum id est Angliae, Scotiae, vicinarum que insula rum ac regionum scriptores vetustio res ac praecipui*, 1587.
   History of the Kings of Britain, translated by Sebastian Evans, Everyman's Library, Dent, London, 1912; revised by Charles W. Dunn, E. P. Dutton & Co., New York, 1958; with an introduction by Gwyn Jones, J. M. Dent and Sons, London, 1963.
   The History of the Kings of Britain, translated by Lewis Thorpe, Penguin Books, Harmondsworth, 1966.

Holinshed, Raphael, *Chronicles* (see General Sources).

Perrett, Wilfrid, *The Story of King Lear from Geoffrey of Monmouth to Shakespeare*, Mayer & Müller, Berlin, 1904.

Tatlock, J. S. P., *The Legendary History of Britain: Geoffrey of Monmouth's Historia Regum Britanniae and its Early Vernacular Versions*, Medieval Academy of America in association with University of California Press, Berkeley, 1950.

THE FLOWER PRINCESS

Baring-Gould, Sabine, "The Gardener Prince", *Old English Fairy Tales*, Methuen & Company, London, 1895.

Child, Francis James (ed.), "The Gardener", *English and Scottish Ballads*, Folklore Press in association with Pageant Book Company, New York, vol. 3, 1957.
   "Patient Grissel", *English and Scottish Ballads*, 8 vols, Little, Brown & Company, and Shepard, Clark and Brown, Boston, vol. 4, 1857.

Greene, Robert, *Pandosto: The Triumph of Time* (also known as *The Historie of Dorastus and Fawnia*), 1588; The Shakespeare Library, Gollancz, London, 1907.

Holinshed, *Chronicles* (see General Sources).

Lyly, John, *The Woman in the Moon*, 1597.

"The Princely Lovers' Garland", *The Roxburghe Ballads*, number 598, vol. 3, circa 1720.

The Royal Courtly Garland, or Joy After Sorrow, broadsheet ballad, 1790.

Sabie, Francis, *The Fisher-man's Tale* and *Of the Famouse Actes, Life and Love of Cassander, a Grecian Knight*, 1595.
   Flora's Fortune: The Second Part and Finishing of the Fisher-man's Tale, 1595.

FURTHER READING

If you want to read Shakespeare's plays, there are plenty of editions published with all sorts of notes and explanations. But some writers have rewritten the plays as stories for children, and even illustrated them to give you an idea of what the plays looked like when they were performed. These include:

Birch, Beverly, *Shakespeare's Stories*, Macdonald Young Books, Hemel Hempstead, 1998.
Garfield, Leon, *Shakespeare's Stories* and *Shakespeare's Stories II*, Victor Gollancz, London, 1985 and 1989.

If you want to read some good factual books that give lots of information about William Shakespeare and his plays, you could try:

Deary, Terry, *Top Ten Shakespeare Stories (with Top Ten Facts)*, Hippo, Scholastic Children's Books, London, 1998.
Ganeri, Anita, *What They Don't Tell You About Shakespeare*, Hodder Children's Books, London, 1996.

And if you like adventure stories or fantasy books, and want to read an exciting story set in Shakespeare's time and about Shakespeare and his friends, you could look out for these novels:

Barlow, Steve, and Skidmore, Steve, *The Lost Diary of Shakespeare's Ghostwriter*, Collins, London, 1999.
Blackwood, Gary, *The Shakespeare Stealer*, Penguin Putnam, Inc., New York, 1999.
Cooper, Susan, *King of Shadows*, Simon & Schuster, New York, 1999.

There are loads of interesting books written about Shakespeare, his life, the lives of his friends, the way people lived in his day, and, of course, about his plays. Keep your eyes and ears open and you'll find them. And remember – you can always tell a good story more than once!

Barefoot Books
better books for children

At Barefoot Books, we celebrate art and story with books that open
the hearts and minds of children from all walks of life, inspiring them to read
deeper, search further, and explore their own creative gifts. Taking our
inspiration from many different cultures, we focus on themes that encourage
independence of spirit, enthusiasm for learning, and acceptance of other
traditions. Thoughtfully prepared by writers, artists and storytellers from
all over the world, our products combine the best of the present with the best
of the past to educate our children as the caretakers of tomorrow.

www.barefootbooks.com